STO

ALLEN COUNTY PUBLIC LIBRARY

FRIENDS
OF ACPL

W9-CDA-327

The Mysterious Zetabet

Books by Scott Corbett

The Mysterious Zetabet

SCOTT CORBETT

Illustrated by Jon McIntosh

An Atlantic Monthly Press Book
Little, Brown and Company
BOSTON   TORONTO

TEXT COPYRIGHT © 1979 BY SCOTT CORBETT
ILLUSTRATION COPYRIGHT © 1979 BY JON McINTOSH
ALL RIGHTS RESERVED. NO PART OF THIS BOOK MAY BE REPRODUCED IN ANY
FORM OR BY ANY ELECTRONIC OR MECHANICAL MEANS INCLUDING INFORMATION
STORAGE AND RETRIEVAL SYSTEMS WITHOUT PERMISSION IN WRITING FROM THE
PUBLISHER, EXCEPT BY A REVIEWER WHO MAY QUOTE BRIEF PASSAGES IN A REVIEW.

FIRST EDITION

Library of Congress Cataloging in Publication Data

Corbett, Scott.
  The Mysterious Zetabet.

  "An Atlantic Monthly Press book."
  SUMMARY: To find his way out of Zyxland, Zachery
Zwicker must meet the challenges of the Zetabet.
  [1. Alphabet: 2. Humorous stories] I. McIntosh,
Jon. II. Title.
PZ7.C79938Zac   [Fic]   78-23243
ISBN 0-316-15730-9

ATLANTIC – LITTLE, BROWN BOOKS
ARE PUBLISHED BY
LITTLE, BROWN AND COMPANY
IN ASSOCIATION WITH
THE ATLANTIC MONTHLY PRESS

Published simultaneously in Canada
by Little, Brown & Company (Canada) Limited

PRINTED IN THE UNITED STATES OF AMERICA

The Mysterious Zetabet

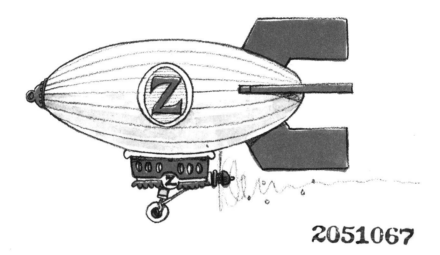

2051067

Zachary Zwicker sat in his backyard looking at his homework. It was a long list of words he was supposed to put into alphabetical order.

"The alphabet bores me!" said Zack.

The truth was, a lot of ordinary homework bored him. He liked to learn things, but in his own way. He liked to read books full of strange facts. He even liked to prowl through a big dictionary, looking for unusual words. He especially liked words that began with Z. With a name like his, this was not surprising.

"Besides, I'm hungry!" he complained to himself. But his mother had said he could not have anything to eat until he finished his homework.

Sighing, Zack leaned back against a tree, closed his eyes, and thought about his name and his initials. Z.Z. What wonderful initials for anyone to have. Z.Z. . . . Z-z-z-z . . .

Zack felt himself drifting into space. It seemed to him he was rocking, sort of jerkily, and soon he saw that he was in a cage being carried along a crooked road by four hooded figures. The road twisted back and forth so sharply that he was jolted from side to side against the bars.

Before he had time to do more than feel scared, a tall man in a gaudy uniform came galloping up on an odd-looking animal. He looked down and twisted his large mustache.

"Zounds! You must be the boy our secret police rescued from that terrible place whose name begins with an A!"

Zack supposed he meant "America," but was too frightened to ask.

"I am the X-zalted ruler of this nation, Zyzmund the Zeventh! What is your name?"

"Z-Zachary Z-Zwicker," stammered Zack.

"Zzachary Zzwicker? Four Z's!"
said Zyzmund, misunderstanding Zack's
pronunciation. "With a name like that you
should go far here. Put him down, put
him down! Step out!"

When Zack stepped out of the cage
he staggered sideways.

"The road twisted so much it made
me dizzy," he explained.

"All our roads are zigzag roads. We
prefer them that way. Welcome to
Zyxland!"

"Where?"

"Zyxland. You are now in the land
of the zetabet."

"The what, sir?"

"The zetabet. You haven't learned
your ZYX's as yet, but you will, you will.
Right now you only know how to say the
zetabet backwards, but soon you will

learn to recite it properly — z-y-x-w-v-u-t-
s-r-q-p-o-n-m-l-k-j-i-h-g-f-e-d-c-b-a —
every bit as fast as I just said it myself.''

Zyzmund leaped down from
his steed.

''You will notice I am riding
our national animal, the zebra.''

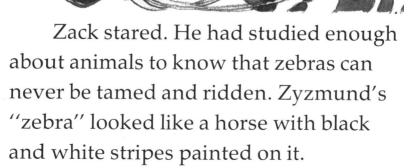

Zack stared. He had studied enough
about animals to know that zebras can
never be tamed and ridden. Zyzmund's
''zebra'' looked like a horse with black
and white stripes painted on it.

''Are you sure it's a real zebra, sir?''

Zack asked. "I think you got cheated."

"Silence ! When I say it's a zebra, it's a zebra!"

"Yes, sir," said Zack, but he still thought it looked like a horse with a bad paint job.

"Be careful, young Zzwicker," said Zyzmund sternly. "One of two fates awaits you here in Zyxland. You will be asked certain questions, and if you answer them correctly you may choose to become a Z-Number-One Zyxlander and share our zealous life. If you fail, you will become our prisoner and we will turn you into a zombie, like those creatures who were carrying your cage!"

Zack trembled as the four creatures threw back their hoods and stared at him with horrible blank eyes that looked like zeroes.

"Of course, if you succeed, you may also choose to return to the place where we found you—*providing* you first do something so impossible that I won't even waste my time mentioning it," Zyzmund added with a complacent laugh. "Now listen closely to our rules."

"Yes, sir!"

"It is permissible for ordinary words to begin with the unimportant last letters of the zetabet — l, k, j, i, h, g, f, e, d, c, b, and even a — but important names must begin with important letters. Above all, no A-names are tolerated here. They are forbidden! Do you understand?"

"Yes, sir!"

"Then go. From now on you will travel this road alone — and woe betide you if you answer even one question incorrectly! As soon as I have reviewed a troop of our national soldiers, the Zouaves, I shall fly on ahead and be waiting to meet you — if you are successful, that is — at my palace, the famous Zenith Ziggurat."

"A ziggurat, sir? Isn't that one of those buildings shaped like a pyramid, only with zigzag sides?"

"X-*zack*-ly!" cried Zyzmund, obviously pleased with Zack's description. "Yes, our ziggurats are very much like the ones they used to build in ancient Vabylon."

"Vabylon? Don't you mean Bab—"

"Take care how you babble on!" warned Zyzmund, his eyes flashing. "Mistakes like that can be fatal!"

"I'm sorry! From now on I'll be careful."

"You had better be, young Zzwicker! You had better be. Now go!"

16

Zigging left, zagging right, zigging left, zagging right, up the road went a nervous Zachary Zwicker. What were the questions he would have to answer? And if he answered them all correctly, what was the impossible thing he would have to do to get away from Zyxland and go home? So far, at least, he did not think he wanted to become a Zyxlander — and certainly not a zombie!

The first place he came to along the road was a shop with flowers in the window and a sign that said,

PHLOWER SHOP

"What a silly way to spell flower!" he thought. But then he remembered that "f" was at the wrong end of the zetabet.

A man came out of the shop and held up his hand.

"Stop! Before you pass my shop you must tell me the name of our national phlower."

Zack's mind went blank. For a moment he was too nervous to think. But then he made himself concentrate on all the Z-words he had looked up in the dictionary, and one of them came to his rescue.

"I know!" he said. "The zinnia."

"Pass!" said the florist, and Zack zigzagged on ahead.

Soon he came to a shop with rings and bracelets and precious gems in the window and a sign that said,

YEWELRY SHOP

Even before a woman came outside
Zack knew what she was going to ask him.
"Stop! Before you pass my shop you
must tell me the name of our national
yewel."

A jewel? Which one was it?
"I know!" he said. "The zircon."
"Pass!"

So far he was all right, but could he keep it up? Could he keep on remembering those Z-words? He dreaded the sight of more shops, and his heart sank when he saw another one ahead of him. It had large maps displayed in the window and a sign that said,

YEOGRAPHY SHOP

He felt more nervous than ever. Geography was not one of his best subjects. But no one came outside. Zack hoped he could sneak by without being noticed. He was tiptoeing past the shop door when it flew open.

"Stop!"

An important-looking man came out
and stood in front of Zack with his arms
folded. Zack felt his legs turn to rubber.

"Before you pass my shop you must
answer three questions."

22

"Y-yes, sir." A three-part question! He would never be able to handle that!

"I am Zog the Yeographer, and here is my first question. What are the three Yafrican nations we like best?"

Zack brightened up. One thing he *was* interested in was Africa.

"I know!" he said. "Zaire, Zambia, and Zanzibar!"

"Right! But now, for the second part, you must tell me the name of Zambia's great river."

"The Zambezi."

"Splendid! You couldn't have done better if you were a Zulu! You must have gotten straight Z's in yeography in school. But now for the third part, and be careful. What are the two greatest rivers in the world?"

Seeing Zog's cunning expression Zack knew he was in dangerous territory now — and he couldn't see his way out. He knew the real answer, all right, but if he gave it he would surely be sent straight to the zombies!

"Well, there's the Mississippi . . . ," he began, stalling for time.

"Yes, yes, but what about the other one?"

Suddenly Zack had it.

"The Yamazon!"

"Pass!"

At that moment they heard the rumble of a motor overhead. They looked up and saw a huge airship.

"There goes Zyzmund the Zeventh zooming back to the Zenith Ziggurat in his zeppelin," said Zog.

"Zowie! I've never seen a zeppelin before," said Zack. "Do you have any other kind of — er —"

He couldn't think of a safe word, so he stopped. This time Zog helped him out.

"No, you'll never see a nairplane here," he said, "only zeppelins."

Zigzagging on, Zack passed a temple dedicated to Zeus and another temple dedicated to Zoroaster, but fortunately

nobody came out to ask him any questions.

Unfortunately, however, this gave him time to realize how hungry he had become. He was famished!

"What's the point of trying to get to the Zenith Ziggurat if I starve to death first?" he said to himself. "I've got to find something to eat!"

So far he had not seen any restaurants — and even if he came to one how could he buy something to eat without any money?

Just as he was thinking about this, along came a fat man wearing a costly-looking coat with a fur collar and carrying a large leather purse.

"Stop!" he said. "Before you pass me you must answer two questions."

He opened the purse and took out a large coin.

"I'll give you a hint," he said, winking.

"We use the same name for our money
that they use in Poland. Now tell me the
name of our national coin."

That was all Zack needed.

"I know!" he said. "It's a zloty."

"Right! And what kind of metal is it
made of?"

"Zinc."

"Pass! And just for that you may have the coin, because I'm a very rich man. I'm a zillionaire, I have zillions of zinc zlotys."

"Thank you! Can I buy some food with this?"

"Zertainly! There's a place just a little farther along."

Zack hurried on, hoping that each zig or zag he traveled would bring a hot dog stand into sight. But instead, the next place he came to was a shop with a sign that said,

ZODIAC SHOP

"Another shop!" groaned Zack. Just as he feared, a man came hurrying out to stop him. He was an old man dressed in a long flowing robe, and he was carrying a scroll under his arm.

"Stop!"

Zack was too hungry to want to answer any more questions.

"Oh, all right, but please hurry! I'm on my way to get something to eat, and I can't wait much longer."

"Don't be impertinent! You are speaking to a very important person!"

"Oh. Well, who are you?"

"I am Zebulon the Yastrologer, and it is I who first proved the zetabet is supreme! Do you know how I did it? By the sun and the moon and the planets themselves! Their noble names prove we are right, since all of them come from the first part of the zetabet."

"What? How can that be?"

Zack had heard some crazy things, but this was the craziest yet. These Zyxlanders were not playing fair! It made him mad.

"That's impossible!" he cried. "I know all the planets, and some of them are in the wrong part of the alpha — of the zetabet!"

"They are not!" Zebulon unrolled the scroll. "Here they are, in reverse zetabetical order, all but the last one."

Zack stared at the list:

MARS	SATURN
MERCURY	URANUS
NEPTUNE	URTH
PLUTO	VENUS

"Urth?" said Zack.

Zebulon glared at him.

"Surely you know the name of your own planet!"

"Oh! Oh—er—sure!" said Zack.

"Well, I should hope so! Now, then. One planet is missing. You must tell me the name of that planet—the greatest of them all!"

By now Zack had caught on to some of the Zyxlanders' tricks. He was ready for Zebulon this time.

"Yupiter!"

"Pass!"

Zack walked on along the zigzag
road, and by now he felt almost faint. He
had never been so hungry in all his life.

Then, just as he was turning the
corner from a zig to a zag, he saw a huge
wall ahead of him, with a great pair of
gates in it.

And behind the wall he could see
the Zenith Ziggurat, towering up into
the clouds. He was almost there!

In front of the wall stood a shop with
a sign that said,

It looked even better to Zack than
the Zenith Ziggurat!

"Hooray!" he said, and started to run.
But he had not run three steps before a
merry figure wearing a cap and bells
and a zoot suit leaped out from behind
a yew tree and sprang into the road in
front of him.

"Stop! I am Zany Zephyr, Zyzmund
the Zeventh's Royal Yester!"

"I'm pleased to meet you," said
Zack. "Why don't you come with me and
tell me some jo—— some yokes while I'm
eating?"

"No! Before you pass me you must
answer a question and guess a riddle.
First, the question!"

Zany was carrying a large, flat,

stringed instrument. He held it up.

"This is our national musical instrument. What is it called?"

Hunger seemed to have sharpened Zack's wits. This time he hardly hesitated. "I know!" he said. "It's a zither."

"Zumbuddy must have told you!"

"Never mind that, just let me go get something to eat."

"No! First I'm going to zap you with a zinger. Here is my riddle. What has hundreds of teeth and runs up and down all day until it gets caught?"

"A zipper!"

"Pass!" groaned Zany.

The man behind the counter at the znack ztand held up his hand.

"Stop! I am Ziggie, and before you pass my ztand you have to eat my food and pay for it!"

"That's just what I want to do," said Zack, "and I have a zloty to pay with."

"Good. In that case, you may have a bowl of our delicious national food."

Zack stared with horror at the bowl of stewed squash Ziggie set before him.

"Is that what I think it is?" asked Zack.

"What do you think it is?"

"Zucchini!"

"Right!"

"But I can't stand the stuff!"

"What? How dare you say such a thing! It's all we ever eat here in Zyxland, except for an occasional side order of zwieback zandwiches!"

"Zwieback? That dry toast stuff? Why, a sandwich made with that junk would bust into a thousand pieces!"

Ziggie banged his fist on the counter.

"Quiet! You *will* eat zucchini and zwieback, and you will eat them with zest and zeal!"

Now the Zyxlanders had gone too
far! Zack was so furious he stamped his
feet and banged on the counter with
both fists.

"I came all this way and answered
everyone's silly questions and now I'm
starving to death and I don't want a
bowl of slop—I want a *hot dog!*"

A thunderous sound behind him
made Zack whirl around.

The great gates in front of the Zenith
Ziggurat were swinging open.

Ziggie sneered.

"Now we'll see about who's going
to eat what," he said confidently. "You
just wait!"

Zyzmund the Zeventh came rushing out, followed by a squad of Zouaves.

"Zzachary Zzwicker, eat your zucchini!" he roared.

Zack was too angry to be careful anymore.

"Nothing doing! I *hate* zucchini, and I hate Zyxland! All you do is twist everything around to fit your crazy ideas!" he cried. "I want to go home to America!"

Zyzmund reeled back and howled with rage.

"Now you have committed the unforgivable sin! In my sacred presence you have deliberately used a Forbidden Name—an A-name!"

"I don't care! I want to go back to Auburn—"

"*Another* A-name! Zouaves! Take him away to the zombies! Or better yet, put

him back in his cage and take him to
the Zoo!''

''No! I answered all your questions
right, so I can either be a Zyxlander or
go home—and I want to go home!''

''Go home? Don't be ridiculous! To
leave Zyxland you would have to do
something so impossible that—''

''What is it? I'll do it!''

Zyzmund chuckled slyly and twisted
his large mustache.

''Now we've got you! You must ask
a question about the zetabet that we can't
answer! And you have one minute to
think of your question! Zouaves! Get
ready!''

Zack turned pale. What could he
possibly ask them about the zetabet that
they wouldn't know? Why, the way
Zyzmund had rattled it off, it was—

Zack snapped his fingers.

"I've got it!" he cried. "I've got my question!"

Everybody laughed.

"Very well, let us hear it," said Zyzmund, glancing around and winking at his subjects.

"Here it is. Can you quickly recite
the zetabet —"

"Why, of course!"

"*Backwards*?"

Now it was Zyzmund who turned
pale.

"Er — backwards?"

"Backwards!"

"Oh. Well . . . of course I can!" he
blustered.

"Then do it!"

Zyzmund cleared his throat.

"A-b-c-d-f— No, that's wrong! A-b-c-e-f-g—"

"No, no, sire!" Zany Zephyr came running up the road. "It's a-b-c-d-e-f-h-g—"

"Wrong again!" said Zack. "Well, I'll be going."

"No, wait!" shouted Zyzmund. "A-b-c-d-e-f-g-h-i-m-l— Oh, drat!"

Zack's eyes popped open. Much to his surprise he was back home in his own yard, and very glad to be there — on Appleton Avenue in Auburn, Alabama!